I0771569

Rico

Book 2

SAMANTHA COLE

To Charles Goodyear (1800-1860),
the inventor of the latex condom.

Rico Demara's thumb hovered over the send button on the text he just typed out. It should've been a no-brainer to say yes to a night of mindless fucking with no strings attached that he occasionally enjoyed with Basil Landry. The two men had been acquaintances for years, following a random hookup one night. Rico wouldn't go so far as to say they were friends since ninety percent of their time together was spent getting each other off. He knew the basics about Basil—his name, age, phone number, his occupation—mechanic—and the fact he never fucked anyone without a condom, nor did he smoke or do drugs. He also had an incredibly talented mouth, but beyond all that, Rico knew little about the man. He had no idea if Basil had brothers or sisters, if he had any family he was close to, or even if he was originally from San Francisco or had grown up somewhere else before moving to the Bay Area. Basil knew just as little about Rico. It's how the two men preferred to keep their relationship. Whenever they both found themselves unattached, they hooked up—plain, simple, and uncomplicated.

Rico wouldn't have hesitated if it was any other night than Wednesday. His staff at the Cock & Bull, the pub he owned, could handle things while he took the rest of the night off, so that wasn't why he wavered in his response to Basil. Nope, the reason why he couldn't press that damn button was because *he* might walk in.

He was a six-foot-two, two-hundred-pound, delicious man named Evan. Rico didn't even know the guy's last name, but that hadn't stopped Rico from lusting after him. Evan came in like clockwork every Wednesday night at six thirty for the past seven weeks. He sat at the end of the bar, ordered a burger or sandwich for dinner, had a few beers, and chatted with the staff and other patrons. If the Giants played a baseball game that night, he watched it on the large-screen TVs above the bar, cheering and groaning with everyone else, depending on whether the local team was winning or losing.

He was in his late thirties, with a fine physique, and was so damn good-looking, he made Rico's mouth water. With light-brown hair, chocolate-colored eyes, and classic features, he garnered the attention of men and women alike but never returned their interest—at least not that Rico had noticed. Evan always seemed a bit shy whenever anyone hit on him, but he never appeared insulted if it was a guy. In fact, Rico knew some of the regulars were trying to figure out whether Evan was gay, straight, or bi without coming right out and asking him. Either way, it wouldn't bother anyone since the Cock & Bull was an all-inclusive establishment catering to many in the LBGTQ+ community.

Over the past year and a half, the C&B had become a popular place for both locals and tourists, no matter their sexual orientation. Occasionally, the bouncers needed to kick out a few bigots, who somehow missed the prominent pride flag in the front bay window, but it didn't happen often.

If Rico had to guess, Evan was in the closet. Several times, while looking through the reflection in the mirror behind the bar, Rico caught Evan eyeing him with a lustful expression that would quickly disappear again before anyone else would notice. Rico even tried a little subtle flirting with the guy last week, but all Evan did was blush, finish his beer, and say he needed to get home.

It drove Rico nuts that he couldn't get a read on the guy, and the last thing he wanted was to be someone's experiment or dirty little secret. But he couldn't stop watching the door and the clock, waiting for Evan to stroll in.

He was just about to say fuck it and hit send on his phone when the object of his growing obsession arrived, looking yummy in faded snug jeans and a royal blue Henley. Evan greeted the hostess, Elena, as he did each week, then headed for an open stool at the end of the bar.

Since the other bartender, Austin Haynes, was busy making some mixed drinks, Rico poured a Coors Light draft, ambled over to Evan, and set it down in front of the man, who chuckled. "Thanks, Rico. If you know what I want before I even order it, I guess this means I'm a regular now."

Rico hated how much it turned him on to hear this man say his name in that rumbling voice that he felt all the way down to his toes. And what was up with his cock's reaction to Evan's statement about knowing what he wanted? If the man knew what Rico really wished Evan wanted from him, he'd probably leave and never come back.

Why the fuck did he have to be attracted to the closeted ones? Been there, done that, had the bruises on his heart to remind him it was a bad idea to get involved with any guy who was too mortified to admit he was into men and not women.

Rico forced himself to treat the hunk like all the other patrons. "Guess so. Want a menu?"

Evan glanced at one of the boards hanging on the walls around the restaurant, announcing the night's specials. "Nah, don't bother. The whiskey burger sounds good—I'll have that. Medium rare, please."

"You got it."

Thankfully, the next few hours were busy because it

kept Rico from constantly ogling Evan, although he had to suffer through watching him get hit on by two men and one woman. Perverse satisfaction stole through Rico when all three were shot down—politely, of course.

Around nine p.m., Rico's friends Scout Turner and Alex Shepherd walked in, surprising him because of the late hour. Scout was a self-made millionaire and the founder and CEO of Turner Continental, which owned several hotels and apartment complexes, including the Paradox Hotel & Residencies across the street from the Cock & Bull. The hotel took up the first twenty-eight floors, while condos occupied the next fourteen. Rico lived on the thirty-second floor, while Scout and Alex's home was one of two penthouses.

He and Scout had known each other since they met when their separate elementary schools were funneled into one middle school. When Rico's parents were killed in a car accident at the end of his sophomore year of high school, he had to move in with his aunt, uncle, and cousins in another school district. Despite that, Rico and Scout stayed close, and Rico thanked God for that friendship on more than one occasion.

In fact, if it hadn't been for Scout, the Cock & Bull would still only be Rico's pipe dream. When Rico had trouble getting a bank loan to open the business, Scout stepped in and became a silent partner. At first, Rico adamantly turned his friend down, but the bastard could be relentless when he wanted something. In the end, the only way Rico agreed to accept the money was if it was considered a loan that he would repay, and thanks to the success of the C&B, he had no trouble making the monthly payments with interest to Scout.

About a year ago, Scout hired Alex as his new personal assistant and winded up breaking his steadfast rule of not dating or fucking any of his employees. Alex had gone high school with Rico's cousin, Gino, but they were both a few years younger than Rico, and he hadn't remembered Alex from school when Scout introduced them. Rico liked to think that a conversation with his friend a few months later prompted Scout to take a chance on love, which the man had finally done. Back in December, right before Christmas, Scout and Alex got engaged while on a trip to New York City. The wedding would take place in October, with Rico being Scout's best man and Alex's sister standing up for him.

Rico was annoyed to feel relieved when Scout and Alex took the two now-empty stools beside Evan on the short end of the bar, hoping it would cut down on the number of people hitting on the man. Evan's stool was in the corner next to the wall, so there was little space for someone wanting to squeeze past the other two men to talk to him.

Tossing two cardboard coasters on the bar in front of Scout and Alex, Rico said, "Hey, what are you guys doing here this late?"

Scout was the one to answer. "Just came from the

art gallery that's handling Rex's exhibition. Tonight was the private showing before the gala on Saturday. You're going, right?"

Rex Adams was a friend of Scout and Rico and a well-sought-after artist as of late. After years of hard work, Rex's career finally took off about twenty months ago. It was after movie star Magnus Keller, who lived in the Paradox penthouse opposite Scout and Alex's, had done a recorded interview from the sanctity of his San Francisco home. When the female reporter asked who the artist was of the stunning painting that hung in his living room, he told her about Rex, whose art also graced some of the walls in the lobby of the hotel downstairs. Rex hadn't even known about the interview until after his phone started ringing off the hook. Since then, his paintings sold like crazy. Canvases that were in storage for years now hung in the homes of some of the wealthiest people around the world. To say the guy was still shell-shocked was an understatement.

"Wouldn't miss it for the world. I'm glad he's finally getting the recognition he deserves." Rico always knew his friend had talent and that it was only a matter of time before everyone else knew it too. In fact, he proudly had two of Rex's paintings on display in his living room, having been gifted them as housewarming presents when he moved into his condo.

"Right. If we knew all it would take was for Mag to open his big mouth, he would've been a hit years ago."

"What can I get you two? The usual?"

Scout glanced at his fiancé, who nodded. "Why break tradition?"

Rico chuckled, then left to retrieve a Guinness draft for Alex and a Grey Goose and club soda with a twist of lime for Scout. By the time he brought the drinks to them, they were involved in a full-blown conversation with Evan about the upcoming NFL draft the following weekend. As Rico set the glasses on the bar, Evan stuck his hand out to Scout. "By the way, I'm Evan Calhoun."

Rico's longtime friend accepted the handshake. "Scout Turner, and this is my fiancé, Alex Shepherd."

Evan shook hands with Alex. "Nice to meet you. Wait a minute. Scout Turner, as in Turner Continental? As in the hotel across the street?"

Both Scout and Alex nodded, and Rico held his breath. Usually, people freaked out and made fools of themselves when they realized they were sitting next to a multi-millionaire—a hotel magnate—but Evan surprised him. "My nephew, Billy, just started working for you—well, for the restaurant there. He's a busboy."

Scout smiled. "Blond hair, tall as hell for a seventeen-year-old?"

Evan's face lit up when he realized the wealthy man beside him knew who a lowly busboy was. "Yeah, that's him."

"He's a good kid and doing a great job."

Sapphire's was the upscale restaurant off the hotel

lobby, and there was rarely a night when it wasn't filled to capacity.

"Thanks. My sister told him that if he wants a car, she'll help him get it, but he has to pay for the gas and insurance. My son, Brian, almost had a heart attack when Billy told him Magnus Keller—you know, the movie star?" When Scout and Alex just smiled and nodded, Evan continued, "Well, he was there for dinner, and Billy said his hands shook anytime he had to refill the guy's water or a breadbasket."

"Mag's a nice guy," Alex said. "But I don't blame your nephew for being starstruck around him. The first time I met him, I couldn't think of a single thing to say to him until Scout made me down a few shots of whiskey. Then I couldn't shut up." His cheeks reddened as his fiancé laughed at him. "It was very embarrassing. Scout doesn't let me forget it, but Mag was cool about it. I'm used to him living across the hall from us now."

While the three men continued to chat about different things, Rico covertly studied Evan. It hadn't escaped his attention that Evan had a son, which made Rico wonder if the man was married or divorced. There was no ring on his left hand and no sign that one was usually worn but had been removed for the night. As he often did on Wednesday evenings, Rico tried to pick up more details Evan might drop about himself. But a small crowd of businessmen and women walked over from a late meeting at the Paradox, crowding around the bar, and Rico needed to focus on helping Austin fill the drink orders.

About an hour later, things were under control again. Most patrons had left for the night, needing a few hours of sleep before tomorrow's workday began. Austin could close up without any problems with the help of Reggie, one of the bar-backs. The kitchen was shut down, and only a few tables lingered, so one waitress and a busboy would stick around until they left.

Scout and Alex stood from their stools as Rico approached them. "Done for the night?"

"Yeah," Scout responded as he left a large tip, which would go into Austin's jar. As the owner of the Cock & Bull, Rico never kept any tips while tending the bar, leaving them for his staff. They worked hard and deserved every penny. "We're flying up to Washington tomorrow to check on things, and we'll be back Friday."

Last year, Paradox North opened in Seattle and was as successful as Turner Continental's other properties. Scout had the golden touch regarding hotels and other business ventures.

"Have fun. I'll see you Saturday."

"Don't forget it's black-tie."

His eyebrows shot up. "Seriously?"

Scout chuckled. "Didn't you read the invite?"

"Just the date and time. Crap, you know I hate wearing freaking ties." Jeans and a sports jacket over a T-shirt were as dressed up as Rico liked to get, even though both men and women told him numerous times over the years that he rocked a suit or tux.

Alex laughed. "You can easily pull off a Frank Sinatra and leave the tie hanging with the top button of your shirt open."

"He does look really fucking sexy when he's being the rebel, doesn't he?" Scout joked to his fiancé, causing Rico to roll his eyes. They didn't have to worry about Alex's reaction to Scout calling Rico sexy. The man knew his future husband was madly in love with him, and even though Rico and Scout both figured out they were gay in high school, they never experimented with each other. It would've been like kissing a brother, and just the thought of it grossed them out. That didn't mean teasing each other wasn't done all the time.

Rico pointed at the door. "Out. Get out. Alex, take him home."

The two men laughed at his expense as they strode toward the door, and Rico just stood there shaking his head. When Evan threw money down on the bar to cover his bill, along with a generous tip, and got to his feet to leave, too, Rico tried to fight back his disappointment. Now he'd have to wait another week to see him again—not that he did anything other than silently lust after the man.

"Well, I'm out of here too. Have a good night, Rico."

"'Night, Evan."

Rico was about to turn away when he noticed the other man hesitate after taking a few steps toward the door. He seemed to have a small battle with himself, and Rico swore he heard him mutter, "Just fucking do it already," before returning to the bar. Rico lifted his brow and waited to hear what the man wanted.

Evan took a deep breath, then asked, "Would you like to . . . I don't know . . . go somewhere for a cup of coffee or something?"

That was the last thing Rico expected the man to say, and he just stared at him for a moment. No one else was at that end of the bar, so their conversation would be just between them. As Rico tried to formulate an appropriate response, Evan ran a hand down his face. "You know what? Never mind. Sorry. I'm not good at this."

Before Evan could turn away, Rico reached across the bar and grabbed his arm, stopping him in his tracks. It took him a few seconds to weigh his words, but the longer he pondered what he wanted to say, the more annoyed he got. Physically, he definitely wanted the other man, but he doubted they were on the same page. "Look, I don't date anyone in the closet, and I refuse to be someone's experiment, so if that's what's going on here, I'll pass."

There was a long pause, and then Evan nodded. "And if it's not? Because I've been out for over a year, and I've already done enough experimenting with guys who didn't mean a thing. I'm done with that. What I meant by not being good at this is I've never asked a guy on a date before." A wry smile ghosted his face.

"Hell, I haven't asked anyone out on a date in about twenty-five years. My ex-wife and I were high school sweethearts."

"You're bi?" Rico had nothing against anyone who was bisexual, but he was only into guys and didn't like dating someone who might want to bring a woman into the mix. He held his breath as he waited for a response.

Two

Evan was fucking this up. The first time he stepped foot in the Cock & Bull was on a Wednesday eight weeks ago when a few people from the radio station where he worked went there for someone's birthday. At some point during the evening, he spotted the hot bartender on the other side of the room from his group's table. After that, he had a hard time keeping his gaze off him. Thankfully, the only one who noticed him ogling the six-foot hunk, with tattoos peeking out from the short sleeves of his black T-shirt, was his friend Lily Albert, who worked in the advertising department at KCXN. She sat beside him and leaned over to whisper, "He's yummy, isn't he? He swings your way, too, and last I heard, he's single. His name is Rico Demara, and he owns the place."

She laughed when Evan stared at her, shocked that she knew all that. "I know his name and that he's the owner because he advertises with us. As for the rest of the info, when I was here last Saturday with a few girl-friends, we flirted with him and another bartender—not the cute blond one working tonight. Anyway, the other guy said we were barking up the wrong tree with Rico. When Donna said she had a friend she could hook Rico up with if he was interested, he said he wasn't dating anyone but also doesn't do blind dates."

"Jesus, woman. Do you know his shoe size too?" was his hoarse response.

She'd smirked. "My guess is he's a size thirteen, which means he probably has a really nice package. His shirt wasn't tucked in the other night, so I can't say for sure, of course."

Evan had practically choked at that.

Since that night, he stopped in every Wednesday for a few hours, attempting to get to know the man better while trying to summon the courage to ask him out. All Rico had to do was say hello, and Evan's knees got weak.

Evan gave himself a deadline to finally ask Rico on a date, and tonight was the night. Now, he wasn't sure if it was a big mistake.

"No, I'm not bi. Just spent twenty years in denial. When I told my wife, she wasn't exactly surprised—said she suspected over the last five years of our marriage that I struggled to admit to myself I was gay. We got divorced last year—amicably—and I came out around the same time. Lost some friends and family members over it, but I'm done trying to convince myself I'm something I'm not." He would've ended his little speech there, but in for a penny, in for a pound, as his grandmother used to say. "As for the experimenting, I hit some clubs after we separated and hooked up with a few guys. Not exactly proud of the fact I never got more than their first names, but I had to make sure, you know?"

He was surprised when Rico nodded. Damn, the man was attractive—like, drool-worthy attractive. His hazel eyes appeared more green than brown tonight, and his dark-brown hair was longer on the top and back, fading to very short on the sides. The five o'clock shadow gracing his jawline and upper lip added to his allure. The gray Cock & Bull T-shirt he wore was taut across his muscular shoulders, chest, abs, and biceps and tucked into a snug and faded pair of blue jeans. And Lily would be happy to know that, under the denim, the man did have a nice-looking package to go with a tight, rounded ass.

"Anyway," Evan continued. "I've been on a few dates recently, but they asked me out. I never . . . look, I like you, Rico. I'm attracted to you and would like to get to know you better. I hoped we could do that somewhere other than where you work. But if you're not interested—"

"I am."

A shiver went down Evan's spine as those two

words, spoken in Rico's deep baritone voice, skirted over his skin. "You are?"

Smirking, Rico chuckled. "Yeah, I am. Give me about ten minutes to take care of a few things before we leave. A coffee shop two blocks away is open all night."

Shocked and a little delirious, Evan nodded and sat back down on the stool. Holy shit. He did it. He finally managed to get the nerve to ask the guy out, and Rico said yes. Wow.

Okay. Play it cool, Ev. Don't rush things or sound desperate. Keep the conversation neutral, and don't talk too much. And for God's sake, stop your hands and knees from shaking like there's a damn earthquake!

As Evan paid for their coffees, Rico picked up the two cups the barista had placed on the counter, then gestured toward an empty table next to the large window by the front door. "Over there, okay?"

Evan nodded like a bobblehead doll. "Um, yeah, that's . . . that's fine."

Rico strode over, trying not to laugh at the other man's apparent nervousness. It had been a long time since Rico was on a date with someone so unsure of himself. He found it endearing.

He set the cups on the table and then decided to be a gentleman and remain standing until Evan joined him before taking a seat. Across from him, Evan took a sip of his coffee. Rico waited silently for a few moments, watching Evan try to think of something to start a conversation with, then took pity on him. "You mentioned earlier you have a kid—Brian, was it?"

A grateful expression crossed Evan's face. "Uh, yeah. Actually, I have two boys. Brian's seventeen, and Mark is fourteen."

"How'd they take the divorce and you coming out?"

Evan shrugged, then his shoulders relaxed. "How does any kid take their folks getting a divorce? It kinda hit them out of the blue. They had no idea there were any problems. In fact, aside from me finally admitting I'm gay, Susan and I had a good marriage. She became my best friend when we started dating during our sophomore year of high school. She still is —she took my announcement better than anyone, including me. I just feel bad that I didn't tell her sooner. She deserves to find someone who can love her in a way I can't. I *do* love her—I always will—but I'm not *in* love with her. I'm not sure if I ever was. Getting married and having kids seemed like what I was supposed to do, you know? Brian and Mark were shocked when I came out to them, but they seem okay with it now. What about you? Have you always known you were gay, or did you have trouble figuring it out?"

Swallowing a sip of his coffee, Rico nodded. "Yeah, I figured it out when I was a freshman in high school.

Ironically, my best friend realized he was gay around the same time."

"Scout?"

"Yeah."

"Did you two ever—" His eyes widened in shock and embarrassment. "Never mind, that's none of my business."

Rico smiled. "Don't worry about it. No, we never hooked up. Never even kissed. We're close—like brothers—and that just felt too weird to even think about. We did talk to each other about what we did with other guys, but that was it."

"How did you two meet?"

"We lived a few blocks away from each other but were in different elementary schools. Those combined into one middle school. He sat beside me in social studies on the first day of sixth grade, introduced himself, and asked if I was a Giants or A's fan. I said I was a diehard Giants fan. He slapped me on the shoulder and said, 'Thank fuck. I thought I was going to have to kick your ass.' I laughed so hard because he was four inches shorter and about thirty pounds lighter than me at the time. Turns out I found the best friend I could ever ask for."

Evan grinned, and Rico couldn't keep his gaze off the man's dimples. They were sexy and turned him on. He subtly shifted his hips, trying to give his hardening cock some breathing room, and steered the conversation to something more serious as a way to get his body back under control.

"Scout was there for me at some of the worst times in my life. At the end of tenth grade, my folks were killed in a car accident. I was an only child. My aunt and uncle, my dad's brother, took me in, and I had to switch school districts because of where they lived. Scout never let me go, though. Despite living across town from each other and going to different schools, he was always there for me."

There were many more occasions when Scout was there to hold Rico's hand and get him through some bad times, and Rico would be forever grateful for his best friend. However, now wasn't the time to get into all of that. He and Evan would have to be a lot farther into a relationship before he would spill his guts about everything he went through since his parents died.

Reaching over, Evan set his hand on the one Rico rested on the table. "I'm sorry for your loss. It's hard at any age to lose your parents, but no more than when you're still a kid."

Rico felt a tingling shoot from his fingers all the way up his arm at the warm touch. He turned his palm over and squeezed Evan's hand before letting go and picking up his cup. "Thanks." He cleared his throat and took another sip of his cooling coffee. "Okay, let's get off the morose topics. I just realized I don't even know what you do for a living."

The tension surrounding them lifted. "I'm a broadcast engineer, otherwise known as a sound technician, for the radio station KCXN. I usually work from six a.m. to two p.m., Monday through Friday, but I occasionally pick up some overtime when other techs call out sick or take vacation."

"So, you work with Bentley and Barrett, the sportscasters? I listen to them every morning."

"Yup, and then I cover Morrison and Savage."

Rico snorted. "Sorry to hear that." When Evan's eyebrows rose and he tilted his head, Rico shrugged. "Sorry, but Savage came into the bar one night—he thinks mighty highly of himself. I wasn't impressed."

Evan toasted him with his cup. "Well, then, that makes two of us. He is a bit of an ass, but you didn't hear that from me."

"Hear what?" he asked with a grin as he touched his cup to the one Evan held up.

They spent about two hours and another round of coffee, talking and getting to know each other on a more personal level. As much as he hated to end the night, Rico knew Evan needed to get some sleep if he had to be at work by six in the morning. "It's getting late. Where did you park? I'll walk you to your car."

God help him, Evan licked his bottom lip before answering him. It stirred up the desire Rico tried to hold at bay all night. What he wouldn't give to invite the other man back to his condo where they could spend hours pleasuring each other. But something in him said Evan was special, and the worst thing he could do was rush things and fall into bed with him for a quick fuck.

"We passed my truck on the way here."

"Great."

They tossed their empty cups into the trash by the door, then stepped out into the night. Their walk was in silence but not uncomfortable. Rico had the urge to reach over and grasp the other man's hand in his, but he hesitated too long because Evan stopped next to a late model Chevrolet Colorado ZR2. "This is me."

Rico eyed the vehicle. "Nice ride."

"Thanks."

When Evan didn't make a move to get into the truck, Rico stepped toward him, forcing the man to back up until his ass hit the door. But Rico didn't stop closing the distance until barely a breath separated them. He studied Evan's face, making certain the man was okay with what was happening. He was relieved to see desire and need in those chocolate-brown eyes. Rico knew if he took one more step, smashing their bodies together, he wouldn't be able to control himself. So, instead, he cupped Evan's jaw, then leaned forward and brushed his lips over Evan's. He wasn't sure if the moan he heard had come from Evan or himself, but he didn't care.

Rico caressed Evan's lips again before pulling the upper one between his own. Evan's mouth was soft and supple as Rico used his tongue to entice him into opening up. When Evan's lips parted, Rico swept in for a taste. When he heard another moan, he knew it had come from Evan. Their tongues slid against each other as they made out on the sidewalk, oblivious to anyone walking by. Evan settled his fists on Rico's hips as if needing to touch him, but knowing if he opened his hands, he'd lose control and be all over him.

Reining in his passion, Rico gave Evan one last sweet kiss before releasing him. Ignoring his hard-on begging for relief, Rico took a step back, pleased to see Evan breathing heavily and licking his lips as if savoring Rico's taste.

Rico was about to say he had a good time tonight, but then an idea occurred to him. "Do you have a tuxedo?"

"Huh?"

He chuckled. "A tuxedo—you know, a penguin suit. You heard Scout and Alex talking about the gala for our friend's art show this Saturday. I was told to bring a date, but I don't have one. I thought maybe you'd like to go with me."

When Evan pursed his lips and hesitated, Rico's heart sank. But then Evan surprised him. "Um, I'd love to go, but I know absolutely nothing about art."

"Who said I knew anything about it?" he asked with a smile. "I'm going because Rex is my friend. If anyone asks what you think about one of his paintings, just say you like the composition and the artist's sense of balance. If there's a contrast between light and dark, you can mention that too."

Evan laughed. "Where did you learn that?"

"Rex told me all that before I went to his first show so I wouldn't feel like an idiot. Scout is also a good person to stand next to—he understands all that shit better than I do, or at least he can fake it enough to sound like he does. Alex and I don't stray far from him at art shows. If someone asks us something about a painting, we pawn the question off on Scout. We've gotten pretty good at it."

"Well, then, yeah, I'm game. I've got a tux too. Splurged on one a few years ago after I had to keep renting one for award shows."

Rico let his gaze roam down Evan's body and back up again. "I bet you look hot in it too."

The man blushed. "I have a feeling I'll pale in comparison to you in one."

Stepping in and brushing his lips across Evan's again, Rico whispered, "I doubt you pale in comparison to anyone, sweetheart. Don't let me hear you put yourself down again. You're sexy as fuck, and I've wanted you since the first night you were at my bar with that group." When Evan's eyes grew wide, Rico nipped at his jaw. "Oh, yeah, I noticed you that night. Pissed me off we were so busy I couldn't get your name and number."

Evan gulped. "Why—why didn't you say anything when I started coming in every week?"

"I picked up on your nervousness."

He quickly put two and two together. "And you thought I was closeted or newly outed."

"Yup. But I'm glad I was wrong. Let me have your phone." Rico moved back and held out his hand. After Evan swiped the screen, he gave him the cell. Rico put in his number and then hit send to connect to his own phone. When it rang in his pocket, he disconnected the call and returned the device to Evan. "The gala starts at eight. It's only a few blocks from here. If you don't mind driving, you can pick me up across the street. My condo is in the Paradox."

"Um, yeah, that sounds great."

With a final peck on the lips, Rico said, "Yes, it does."

Three

"Hey, Dad? Where are you?"

Evan's hands froze where they'd been straightening his bowtie. He stood in front of the mirror in his bedroom, putting on the final touches to his black tuxedo, and the last thing he expected was for Brian to stop by his apartment. When Susan and Evan decided to divorce, he found a two-bedroom place only ten minutes away from the house they'd shared so he could still be nearby for his sons. While he had the boys over for dinner every Tuesday and Thursday, and they stayed with him every other weekend, he told them they could come over any time they wanted to visit. He was still very active in their lives, going to their baseball and lacrosse games, taking them to the movies or fishing, and giving them rides any time they needed, among other things. He and Susan even went together with Brian to look at different colleges. Susan also invited him over for dinner almost every Sunday. Evan knew, as far as divorces went, he'd gotten damn lucky. His ex-wife was one hell of a woman, and he'd be forever grateful for her understanding and compassion over the end of their marriage.

The lanky seventeen-year-old strolled into the bedroom and looked his father up and down. "Where are you going all dressed up? Another awards show?"

"Uh, no. I'm going to . . . um, an art show."

Brian sat on the edge of the queen-sized bed. "Art show? In a tux?"

"Yup. It's a black-tie party at a gallery downtown." He double-checked the cufflinks he put on earlier, then turned around and held out his hands. "How do I look?"

His son shrugged. "Good, I guess."

"Thanks—I think. What're you doing here anyway? Not that I mind you stopping by."

Brian hesitated a moment, and then his gaze fell to the floor. "Mom let me borrow the car. She's got a date tonight."

Ah. Evan had encouraged Susan to start dating again, but she kept saying she hadn't found anyone she was interested in yet. As far as Evan knew, this would be her first date since their divorce.

He took a seat next to Brian. "Do you know who it is?"

"Nope. She said she'd introduce him to us if he was still around after a few dates."

Taking a deep breath, he let it out slowly. "This is a good thing, Bri. I know it's hard for you and Mark to think about your mom with someone other than me. But she deserves to be happy with someone who can care for her when you and your brother go off to college and the great beyond."

"I know. It's just weird." He glanced at Evan's tux again. "Are you going on a date too?"

When he finally sat his boys down and told them he was gay and it was the reason why he and Susan were divorcing, Evan swore he would never lie to them again. He'd lied to everyone and himself for years, which hurt them all. After they overcame the initial shock, he was surprised by how accepting they were. Times were changing, he guessed. While there were still plenty of people out there who hated the LGBTQ+ community, being gay didn't have the same stigma it had many years ago, especially in the Bay Area.

"Yeah, I am. First date. Well, second—we had coffee the other night."

"What's his name?"

"Rico Demara. He owns a bar and restaurant downtown. It's his friend's art show we're going to."

When Brian just nodded, Evan clasped his shoulder and pulled him close for a sideways hug. "You can hang out here tonight if you want. There's leftover pizza in the fridge."

He shrugged again. "Maybe."

"Where's your brother?"

"At some girl's birthday party."

Evan stood and grabbed his wallet, keys, and phone from his dresser. "None of your friends are doing anything tonight?"

"Nothing I feel like doing. I thought maybe you'd want to go to a movie or something, but it's no big deal." He got to his feet and headed for the door.

Evan followed him. Brian's sullen attitude bothered him, but he knew better than to push too hard to find out why. Teenagers' mood swings for inane reasons were common. "Tell you what—let's give your mom a break from cooking tomorrow and go to Chili's for dinner, and then we'll see the new James Bond movie. Sound good?"

Brian's face lit up with a hopeful expression. "It would sound better if we saw that new horror movie, *Evil Lies Within.*"

"Mom hates horror movies—so does your brother."

"But you love them as much as I do. We can split up."

He considered that for a moment. "All right. If your mom's cool with it, they can go see whatever they want, and we'll see *Evil Lies Within.*" A glance at his watch told him he was going to be late. "Shoot, I've gotta run." He put his hand on the back of Brian's head and kissed his forehead. "Love you, kiddo. I'll talk to you tomorrow. Lock up when you leave."

"'Kay. Have a good time."

"Thanks."

"Holy crap. Is that Magnus Keller talking to Scout and Alex?" Evan whispered to Rico, who chuckled as they strolled into the gallery after showing their invitation to the bouncers at the door. Yup, big, burly men blocked the door from anyone wanting to get in without the proverbial golden ticket. The large gallery buzzed with men in tuxes and women in gowns, talking and checking out the art on the walls that probably cost more than Evan made in a year. Champagne flutes and hors d'oeuvres were passed around by a smartly dressed waitstaff.

"Yeah. Want to meet him?"

He shook his head almost violently. "No . . . not yet. I think I need a drink before that happens. I'd probably trip over my own tongue."

Rico leaned over, gave him a swift kiss on the mouth, and then laughed at Evan's blush. "I'd rather be the one tripping over your tongue." He took Evan's hand and gave it a gentle tug, gesturing toward a bar tucked into one corner of the main room. "C'mon. A drink first, and then we'll rub elbows with the movie stars."

"There are more celebrities here?" He glanced around, trying to see if he recognized anyone else famous. He spotted the mayor of San Francisco and the placekicker for the 49ers, both with their spouses. A female CBS news correspondent chatted with a man who looked familiar, but Evan couldn't place him.

Rico subtly pointed to Evan's right. "There's Raven Fairbanks and Tyler Brooks."

Evan's steps slowed, and his eyes widened at the sight of one of the most prominent Hollywood couples of the decade. "Holy shit," he muttered. "Do you know them?"

"Nah. In fact, aside from Rex, Magnus, Scout, Alex, and a few others, I've never met most of these people."

Evan was surprised by that since Rico looked like he fit right in with the Hollywood crowd. Dressed in a fitted tuxedo with a dark-blue jacket with black lapels over black pants, he could've walked off a movie set or right out of a commercial for Armani or Christian Dior. The longer strands of hair that usually hung down the center of the back of his head were pulled up into a small ponytail. He hadn't bothered shaving his five o'clock shadow, and it was sexy as hell.

"What would you like to drink, babe?"

A warm feeling spread throughout Evan's body at the endearment falling from Rico's kissable lips. Damn, if he had any questions about whether he was gay or not, they would've fled his mind as Evan imagined Rico's mouth around his cock. Evan didn't care what movie stars were in the room. The man he wanted more than anything in the world stood right in front of him. He mentally shook his head, realizing that Rico and the bartender were waiting for his answer.

"Um, a gin and tonic with a twist of lime would be great," he told the pretty woman behind the bar.

"Certainly. And for you, sir?" she asked Rico.

"Make it two."

A few minutes later, with drinks in hand, they walked around the room, skirting partitions that created more walls to hold the displayed artworks. Rico stopped next to a man standing in front of a huge painting and talking to two women. The man was about two inches taller than Rico, and his shoulders were broader. His chestnut brown hair was cut short, as were his mustache and goatee. When the man's gaze shifted, he saw Rico, and a grin spread across his face before his attention returned to his companions. "Ladies, it's been a pleasure talking to you. If you'll excuse me, I must greet my other guests."

The women looked disappointed but still nodded, said goodbye, and walked away. The man turned, and instead of shaking Rico's hand, he pulled him into a bear hug and slapped him on the back. "Dude, I thought you were going to blow me off."

Rico scoffed as he stepped back. "When have I ever blown you off?"

The man tapped a finger over his closed lips and looked deep in thought for a moment before he laughed loudly. "Um, you've never blown me. Let's keep it that way, shall we? Who's this?"

Rico set a hand on his date's shoulder. "This is Evan

Calhoun. Evan, this is my friend and the man of the hour, Rex Adams."

Rex held his hand out, and Evan shook it. "It's nice to meet you, Rex. Rico's told me a lot about you." He gestured to the large painting they stood next to. "You're a very talented artist."

"Thank you, Evan. Tell me—what do you think about this piece? Be honest."

Evan gulped. Talk about being put on the spot. He tried to remember what Rico told him to say if anyone asked him about a painting. "Um. I like it a lot. Your . . . um, your sense of composition is great."

When Rico and Rex burst out laughing, embarrassment flooded Evan until he realized he was set up. Rico squeezed his hand in apology. "It's 'sense of balance.'"

Still chuckling, Rex shook his head. "I'm just busting your chops, Evan. Trust me, Rico doesn't know what 'sense of balance' means any more than most of the people here do."

"Don't tell me you're embarrassing the poor guy." Scout sidled up to them with Alex by his side. "Give him a break."

Alex grinned at Evan. "Don't worry—they did that to me the first time I met Rex too. I don't know a thing about art either. My go-to phrases now are 'It's a beautiful composition' and 'The contrast is remarkable.' Anything beyond that, I defer to Scout."

"He doesn't know much more than that either, but

he can fake it like the best of them," Rex said as he shook hands with the two newcomers.

"From the sounds I hear coming from their apartment, I don't think Scout is faking it." Magnus Keller slapped Rex's shoulder as he joined the little group.

Laughter bubbled up again, and Alex's cheeks burned red while Scout rolled his eyes. "He can't hear shit, baby. I made sure the insulation between our place and his was triple what was required for that reason alone. I don't need to hear him with his flavor of the week."

Magnus's famous smile spread across his face before he noticed Evan. He held out his hand, and Evan hoped his palm wasn't sweaty when he took it. "Hi, I'm Magnus Kell—"

"I know!" Everyone chuckled while Evan dropped his chin in mortification. Taking a deep breath, he tried to fix his blunder. "Sorry about that. What I meant to say was, hi, I'm Evan Calhoun. It's nice to meet you, Mr. Keller."

"Good to meet you too, Evan, and it's Mag, please." He gestured to Rico and leaned toward Evan conspiratorially. "For the record, he's a keeper."

Beside Evan, Rico groaned. "Shut it, Mag."

"What? It's been ages since I've seen you out on a date. I'm happy for you." He turned back to Evan. "What do you do for a living?"

"I'm a broadcast engineer for KCXN Sports Radio."

"Really? I listen to them all the time when I'm in

town. Don't tell me you work with that asshole, Savage."

"Yup, he does," replied Rico. His gaze met Evan's. "See, I'm not the only one who thinks he's an ass."

Mag put a hand on Evan's shoulder and leaned down to look him in the eye. "Let me tell you what that dickhead did when I ran into him at . . ." He filled Evan in on an incident in a luxury suite at Levi's Stadium before a 49ers' football game. Once again, someone proved what a jerk Dave Savage was. Evan never liked the guy, who was a homophobe, but he usually kept that to himself since Savage was the "talent." If anyone lost their job over a skirmish between them, it would probably be Evan.

The rest of the night out was more comfortable than Evan had expected. Mag was a really nice guy and made Evan feel welcome in their group, as did the others. Rico never strayed more than a few steps away from Evan, except for a trip to the restroom. As the evening wore on, Evan felt as if he'd known Rico's friends forever. They were a great bunch, joking and regaling Evan with funny stories of their times together. He learned a bit more about art from Rex until the man had to mingle with the other guests looking to purchase one of his pieces. A few times, Evan found himself deep in a conversation with Alex, finding the man was easy to talk to—he was someone Evan could see becoming a good friend.

Unfortunately, several friends and family members

turned their backs on him after he came out of the closet—people he thought would stick by him through thick or thin. It hurt to realize how wrong he'd been about them. But now that he started rebuilding his life, he discovered how much he didn't miss those people. This was who he was now—who he always should've been. The only reason he didn't regret exploring his sexual attraction to men at an earlier age was his two sons. Even though he lived a lie for years, one look at Brian and Mark told him it was a mistake he would've done over again in a heartbeat.

As they talked and wandered around the gallery, Rico introduced Evan to a few other people he knew and constantly reminded Evan he was there on a date with him by touching him in subtle ways. Sometimes, it was a brush of his fingers against Evan's or placing his splayed hand on Evan's back. Then, there were a few PG-13 kisses when they occasionally found themselves alone. So far, it was everything Evan had hoped a date with Rico would be, but as they said their goodbyes to everyone, he was nervous about how the night would end. Would Rico invite him in for a nightcap? Or would he tell Evan he had a good time, but he'd see him around?

After they left the gallery, he got his answer when they reached his truck, and in a flash, Rico had him pinned to the side of it, smashing his mouth down on Evan's. Rico's hands held Evan's head in place, and he positioned one of his legs between Evan's. There was no mistaking Rico's hard-on rubbing against Evan's hip, just shy of his own erection.

Evan moaned as his arms encircled Rico's waist, pulling him closer as if that was even possible. They were chest to chest, pelvis to pelvis, in the middle of a municipal parking lot around the corner from the gallery. Rico inhaled him as his tongue plunged into Evan's mouth.

"Get a room," someone said with a chuckle from nearby as they walked past.

Rico eased his mouth from Evan's before barking, "Fuck you, Scout."

"Not in this lifetime, my friend. Have a good night." The amusement in the man's voice was hard to miss.

Evan tried to catch his breath as his heart pounded in his chest. He stared into Rico's passion-heavy eyes. Rico gently rubbed a thumb over Evan's swollen mouth and whispered, "Come home with me."

There was no question about his response.

<h1 style="text-align:center">Four</h1>

As they rode the residents' elevator up to the thirty-second floor of the Paradox, Rico silently cursed John and Sheila Loxley for having shit timing and ending up on the lift with him and Evan. The elderly couple lived on the floor above Rico and were very friendly, which was the only reason he hadn't snarled like a rabid animal when they got on the elevator with them. All he wanted to do was get his hands back on Evan and get him naked as fast as possible. It'd been hard enough not to drag him out of the backdoor of the gallery and attack him in the alley. The man was sexy as sin in his tuxedo, and Rico had fought to keep his cock under control all night. When Evan agreed to come home with him, Rico almost came in his pants right then and there.

"You boys look very handsome tonight," Mrs. Loxley said with a knowing smile.

"Thank you," they responded simultaneously before Evan glanced at Rico. That blush Rico loved was back. He was surprised at how accepting Evan was of the public displays of affection Rico doled out. Rico had expected him to be shy or uneasy about holding hands or the pecks he dropped on Evan's mouth throughout the night since he admitted he'd never been on an actual date with another man since coming out. Rico had been worried about that ever since he invited Evan to the gala with him. Having been out and proud for years, Rico usually avoided men who weren't comfortable with their sexual orientation. In fact, he couldn't explain why he was so drawn to Evan, knowing he'd only recently accepted who he was and what gender his body wanted. He also couldn't determine why he was jealous of the men Evan hooked up with during his experimentation phase. It was almost twenty years since Rico had been another guy's first sexual encounter with a man, but he found himself wishing he could've been Evan's.

When the elevator finally dinged their arrival on Rico's floor, he politely said goodnight to the Loxleys and led Evan to the door to his unit. The condo was something else he had Scout to thank for. There was no way he would've been able to afford the $700,000+ price tag the condos in the building started at while being built a few years ago. But Scout told him to pick out what unit he wanted and refused to take no for an answer. Once again, the man had looked out for his best friend. Some might think charity or pity drove Scout to give his less fortunate buddy the loan to start the bar and a place to live instead of making money off the condo. But Scout never made Rico feel that way.

Despite not being blood-related, the two men were the brothers neither were blessed with. Scout's only siblings were his twin sisters, and Rico was an only child. When Scout became a self-made millionaire, he ensured his family was well taken care of—including his best friend. Rico would never take Scout for granted, though. He paid the man back in both profits from the Cock & Bull and loyalty. Scout could call him up tomorrow and tell him he'd killed someone, and Rico would help him bury the body, no questions asked. He owed him that much.

Unlocking the door, he pushed it open and gestured for Evan to enter before him. He barely gotten the door shut behind them when he found himself plastered up against it with Evan's tongue in his mouth and his hands unbuttoning Rico's jacket and shirt. Rico practically ripped off his bowtie before fumbling with Evan's own buttons. Their tongues dueled as their teeth and lips clashed.

Panting, Rico grasped the sides of Evan's head and pulled him back a few inches. "Last chance to walk away."

Instead of verbally responding, Evan ran his hands up Rico's torso, under the opened sides of the dress shirt, to his shoulders, pushing the shirt and jacket down his arms where they got stuck due to the cuff-links still at his wrists. Evan's hands then dropped to Rico's pants and quickly undid the button and zipper. When his fingers wrapped around Rico's hard length, Rico's legs almost buckled underneath him.

Reaching out, he palmed the back of Evan's head, pulling him in for another powerful kiss that left them both gasping for air.

"Bedroom," Rico managed to mumble before grabbing Evan's arm and dragging him in that direction. Once there, Rico kicked off his shoes and yanked his jacket and shirt off, sending the cufflinks flying, before shucking his pants and underwear.

"Get rid of your clothes," he growled at Evan, who stood frozen while watching him with lust in his eyes.

Impatient, Rico dropped to his knees and made quick work of Evan's pants and boxer briefs, shoving them both down his legs while the man removed his shirt and jacket. Rico didn't give Evan a chance to get rid of his shoes and kick his pants and underwear off from where they were wrapped around his ankles. He filled his hands with the man's ass cheeks, kneading them and pulling him closer to nuzzle the short, curly, coarse hair at the base of his twitching cock.

When Rico ran his tongue up the pulsating vein on the underside of Evan's shaft, a harsh hiss was the response he received before Evan grabbed the small ponytail at the back of Rico's head, holding him there. "Suck me, Rico. Please!"

The desperation in Evan's voice spurred Rico on. Opening his mouth, he engulfed Evan's cock, taking him to the back of his throat. Bobbing his head up and down, Rico licked and sucked the engorged, hard flesh. When a bead of pre-cum hit his tastebuds, he moaned at the salty, bitter flavor. He felt Evan's legs quiver as they fought to keep him standing, and Rico reluctantly released him. "Get on the bed. On your back. I'm not done with that delicious cock yet."

Evan cursed and pinched the base of his shaft, probably to stave off an impending orgasm, as he awkwardly shed his shoes, pants, and briefs before climbing onto the bed. Rico retrieved a bottle of lube and some condoms from the top drawer of his nightstand and tossed them on the bed. He saw a flash of uncertainty steal over Evan's face. Rico froze as worry shot through him. "You said you've been with other men."

Biting his bottom lip, Evan nodded. "I have, but only blowjobs or with me topping. I haven't . . . I mean . . ."

The man gulped nervously, and understanding and satisfaction filled Rico. "You mean no one's taken that hot ass of yours?" When Evan nodded, Rico asked, "And now?"

There was no hesitation this time. "I want you inside me. I want you to fuck me like no one else ever has."

"Shit." Rico crawled up Evan's naked body, letting

their erections rub together as he devastated the man's mouth with his own.

Hands were everywhere, stroking, exploring. Rico nipped along Evan's stubbled jaw until he reached his ear. "I'll go slow, baby. It'll be uncomfortable at first, but I'll make sure you're begging me for relief before long."

Evan put his hands on either side of Rico's face and pushed him back so he could look into his eyes. "I trust you."

Rico was humbled more in that moment than he'd ever been in his life. He kissed Evan, almost reverently, until the man began to squirm under him. Evan's hands gripped Rico's ass and squeezed. Rico ground his pelvis against Evan's, and his hips bucked hard when he felt one of Evan's fingers delve into the crease between his cheeks and ghost over his puckered hole.

Shifting, Rico nuzzled, licked, and nibbled his way down Evan's neck, chest, and abs. The legs beneath him spread wider, giving him room to settle between them. He hoped Evan had no plans for the morning because Rico would spend the entire night worshiping the man's body.

Leaning up on his elbows, Evan watched his cock disappear into Rico's mouth, and he fought the urge to pump his hips upward. Rico laved his length in wet heat, alternating between sucking hard and gently. He cupped Evan's balls, rolling them before teasing the sensitive spot behind them with his fingers.

When Rico took him to the back of his throat and swallowed, Evan cried out over how incredible it felt. He fell back onto the bed and begged unashamedly. "Please, please, not—not yet. Don't make me come yet. Oh, fuck . . . I want you inside me. Please."

Rico's mouth released him, and Evan immediately mourned the loss. But then Rico put his hands on the backs of Evan's thighs, pushing them toward his chest. Evan almost laughed out loud when he realized he still wore his black socks, but the humor fled him when lube-covered fingers caressed his hole. He instinctively clenched his ass.

"Relax, baby. I'll be gentle until you're ready to take me."

Evan forced the tension from his muscles and held his breath as Rico's blunt fingertip eased into him before easing back out. There was some pain—he knew there would be—but it wasn't unbearable. When Evan grabbed the back of his knees and held them, Rico repeated the motion. "Breathe, Evan. Take a deep breath and bear down."

When he did as he was told, Evan felt the finger inside him slide in even farther, but it still hadn't breached his sphincter. It continued to lube his entrance as Rico leaned down and licked Evan's softening cock, quickly bringing it back to life before sucking it into his mouth again. Evan thrust his hips up, shoving his shaft deep into Rico's throat. When Rico swallowed, Evan saw stars, which was the distraction needed for Rico to put more pressure on his finger until Evan's body collapsed around it, granting him entry. The sharp sting drew a hiss from Evan, and he was thankful Rico stilled his finger to allow him to adjust to the newness of having something up his ass. Rico continued to bathe Evan's cock with his tongue, sucking on the tip before enveloping him in delicious warmth.

As the rigidity eased from Evan's body again, Rico moved his finger in a caressing motion inside him while still focusing on giving Evan the mother of all blowjobs. When a second finger was added to the first, Evan wasn't sure how he would be able to take Rico. But then Rico brushed over something deep inside his ass, and Evan nearly hit the ceiling. He never had his prostate stroked before, and it was unlike any explanation he ever heard. In fact, he couldn't describe it even if he tried, but he didn't care. All he wanted was for it to happen again. "Oh, shit! Damn, do that again! Please!"

Rico continued to slide in and out of him, adding a scissoring motion and only hitting that secret spot every few strokes. Evan knew it was to keep him from being overtaken by his impending orgasm.

Pulling his mouth away from Evan's sensitive cock, Rico donned one of the condoms and put a generous amount of lube over his covered length. He stroked himself a few times, then ran his hand over Evan's erection, leaving behind some of the slick substance. "Turn over, baby. It'll be easier if I take you from behind the first time." Once he was in position, on his hands and knees with his ass up in the air, Rico said, "Jack off for me, and remember to breathe."

Evan wrapped his palm and fingers around his cock and tugged while Rico ran his soothing hands up and down Evan's back and over his ass cheeks before parting them. Something thick and hard began pushing against his hole and split him open. "Oh, shit! Rico, it's —it's too much."

"No, it's not, baby. Breathe." His arm came around Evan's hips, and Rico closed his hand over Evan's, encouraging him to drag it up and down his shaft. "Bear down."

Evan did his best to follow the softly spoken order, and when he did, his hole collapsed, allowing Rico access to his dark passage. With a swift thrust, Rico was deep inside him but then held himself still, giving Evan a moment to recover when he cursed up a storm. Once the pain began to ebb and turn into pleasure, Evan realized he needed Rico to move. "Fuck me, Rico. Please."

Grasping Evan's hips, Rico started a tortuously slow pace. The sensations rocketing through Evan caused him to moan and beg for more. As Rico sped up, the sounds of flesh slapping against flesh echoed throughout the room. Once again, Evan began to work his cock with his hand.

"You're so tight," Rico said with a growl. "Feels so good, baby. So good. I'm not going to last long."

Suddenly, Rico adjusted his angle, and the tip of his cock hit Evan's prostate. This time, there was no holding back. Evan's body exploded with such an intense orgasm that he thought for sure he'd pass out when spots appeared before his eyes, and his brain short-circuited. He shouted Rico's name as streams of cum shot onto his hand and the comforter underneath him. Behind him, Rico pounded into Evan's body a few more times, then went deep, stiffening and roaring his release. For a moment, Evan silently cursed the condom the other man wore. He'd give anything to feel Rico marking him in the most primal way.

Unable to prop himself up on his hands and knees any longer, Evan slid forward slowly, making sure Rico stayed inside him until he was flat on the bed. He couldn't even be bothered worrying about the cooling semen that coated his stomach and chest.

Rico leaned down and kissed where Evan's shoulder met his neck, his heavy breathing loud in Evan's ear as he fought to bring it under control. "That was incredible. I don't think I've ever come that hard before."

A smile spread across Evan's face as he glanced over his shoulder. "Same here. I hope you have a washer and dryer in the condo because I made quite a mess on your bed."

Chuckling, Rico slowly withdrew from Evan's body, removed the condom, and tied it off before tossing it in a nearby wastebasket. "You can make a mess like that anytime you want."

Five

Sunlight filtering between closed blinds on the windows awakened Evan, and it took a moment to remember where he was. It wasn't hard to figure out since he was still cuddled into Rico's side, and the man's scent filled Evan's nose.

"Mmm. What time is it?" Rico muttered as he pulled Evan closer.

He noticed a clock on the nightstand. "Just after nine."

Rico's eyelids slowly opened. "I thought it was later than that. We were up pretty late."

That was an understatement. After Rico fucked him senselessly, they took a shower together, which resulted in another orgasm for both of them as Rico wrapped his big hands tightly around both their cocks and jerked them off. Then they ambled into the kitchen, where Rico cooked them omelets. Once their stomachs were satisfied, Evan ended up on his knees, giving Rico a blowjob that had him practically yelling the building down. Rico then returned the favor. They finally dozed off around three-thirty, completely sated and exhausted.

"Do you have plans tonight?" Rico asked as he stretched. "I'd love to see you again."

"Yeah, sorry. On Sunday evenings, I usually have dinner with Susan and the kids. I promised Brian we could eat tonight and then go to a movie he wants to see. But I don't have to be there until around five."

"I've got to open up the bar at ten thirty. It's going to be a busy day with two back-to-back baby showers. We set them up on the second floor and still have room for the lunch crowds. And with the Giants-Yankees game at four in New York, we'll be packed by the time it starts here at one. Mondays and Tuesdays are usually my nights off. It's slow enough, and I trust my staff to handle things. It also helps that I live right across the street."

"How about dinner tomorrow night, then?" Evan kissed the tattoo on Rico's shoulder that extended down his arm. He finally got a good look at it last night in the shower. It was a stunning portrait of a Native American—a tribute to his mother's grandfather, a Chinook tribesman. The tattoo on his other arm consisted of three intertwined flags, a testimony to his other Irish, Italian, and American heritages. He joked last night, saying he was a bit of a mutt. Out of curiosity, he did one of those DNA tests last year and found out that, besides Native American, Irish, and Italian, he also had some Swedish and a small percentage of Welsh ancestry. All combined, Rico was an attractive man—one Evan couldn't wait to get to know even better.

"Sounds good. Why don't you come here? We can eat at Sapphire's."

"I've never eaten there, but I've wanted to. I heard the food is amazing."

Rico propped himself up on one arm and pushed Evan onto his back before kissing him soundly. "Is six thirty okay for you?"

"Perfect."

A smile spread across Rico's face, and he gyrated his hips, grinding his morning wood against Evan's. "Shower with me before you go?"

"Absolutely."

Two-and-a-half weeks later . . .

Rico was in better spirits than he'd been in a very long time. He and Evan had been on several dates and enjoyed talking and getting to know each other better. This past Monday, they went to Sapphire's for dinner again, then took their dessert back to Rico's place, but they never got around to eating it, feasting on each other instead. Rico was disappointed to awake alone the following morning, but Evan needed to be at work at the ass-crack of dawn. Tuesday, they hadn't seen each other but talked over the phone that night, which turned into a round of phone sex, something Rico hadn't done in ages. His new man had a filthy mouth on him when he got going, and Rico loved it.

Last night, Evan made his weekly Wednesday appearance at the bar, and at one point, Rico dragged him back to his private office, where he let Evan fuck his ass. When they reappeared a little while later, Austin, who was tending the bar, quietly winked and grinned at them, clearly figuring out what they'd been doing back there. Evan blushed at the teasing the man gave them, which caused Rico to fall a little more for the guy. Nothing about Evan bothered him—he was good-looking, kind, intelligent, and tidy without being a neat freak. He could hold his own in conversations on a variety of subjects and was as voracious about sex as Rico was. Rico could fuck him all day, every day, and still not grow tired of him.

Before he left the bar last night, Evan asked Rico to come with him for dinner at his ex-wife's house on Sunday. Apparently, Susan told Evan to extend the invitation, and he also wanted to introduce Rico to his kids. While the thought of meeting Evan's family should've scared him, Rico realized he was excited about it. Every day, his feelings for the man grew exponentially.

Right then, though, he looked forward to everything he would do to Evan tonight when he finally got him alone again. The images in his head made his cock twitch in his jeans.

It was just after three p.m., and he sat at the short end of the bar, going through the receipts for the first half of the week and sorting them for the bookkeeping he needed to do later. The lunch crowd had filtered out, and only three occupied tables were left while a handful of people sat at the bar. His daytime bartender, Ashley Beckham, and waiter, David Ripps, had everything covered. They had another hour and a half before their reliefs came on duty, just in time for the happy hour crowd.

Sitting on the bar beside his paperwork, his cell phone dinged with an incoming text message. Rico swiped the screen to read it.

EVAN

Sorry, but I have to cancel tonight. Another sound tech called in sick so they asked me to cover his shift. I'll be here until 10 and have to be back by 6.

He told Rico he didn't get overtime often but picked it up whenever possible because the extra pay was good. Rico understood. Many of his jobs over the years were for hourly wages. When that time-and-a-half rolled around, it was like getting a bonus, so you grabbed it when you could.

Picking up the phone, he quickly typed in a reply.

> No worries. Tomorrow then? You can come to the bar and when things die down, we can head out.

They'd only planned to have dinner at Evan's. Rico looked forward to seeing where the man lived. They'd blessed every room in Rico's condo, and he wanted to do the same at Evan's apartment. Evan said it was a small two-bedroom unit in a quiet neighborhood. When he mentioned it was nowhere near as nice as Rico's place, Rico explained how he could "afford" the expensive condo. Scout held the mortgage, which was far less than anyone else's in the Paradox. Rico also paid the utilities for the unit, but he had free parking in the garage. When he spilled his guts about all that, he was surprised to see some relief in Evan's eyes. It was as if he preferred Rico not to be as rich as his mailing address might indicate.

EVAN

> Sure. I miss you though. I'll call you later when I get a break.

A warm feeling filled Rico. Now he understood why Scout had gotten that goofy look on his face when he'd been falling for Alex.

> Miss you too. TTYL

As he set the phone on the bar, he heard the front

door open and glanced over his shoulder to see who was coming in. A teenage boy wearing jeans, a T-shirt, and sneakers entered and glanced around. When his eyes fell on Rico, there was a flash of recognition . . . and anger?

Rico eyed the kid as he closed the distance between them. He was tall and lanky, with light-brown hair that needed a trim and dark eyes. His mouth was taut, and his jaw tight. Rico noticed his clenched fists as he stopped next to him. "You Rico Demara?"

Yup, definitely anger there. Rico just didn't know why. He never saw the kid before and had no idea who he was.

"Yeah, can I help you?"

"You can stay away from my father. That's what you can do."

Since the bar was quiet, sans a few low conversations and the music filtering through the sound system, the kid's voice traveled, and several people turned to see what the problem was. As he studied the teen's face, Rico realized who he reminded him of—this had to be one of Evan's boys, Mark or Brian. Rico couldn't remember which was older, but the one in front of him appeared to be around seventeen.

"I see. And you are?"

"Brian Calhoun." Disgust filled his face. "What? You're dating more than one guy who has kids?"

Rico spun the stool a little until he faced Brian. "No,

I just wasn't sure if you were you or your brother, Mark. Does Evan know you're here?"

The kid's shoulders stiffened at the mention of his father's name. "Doesn't matter," he spat. "Just leave him alone. He deserves a lot better than you."

When Brian turned to leave, Rico grabbed his arm, not letting the teen yank free. "Calm down. What the hell is this about?"

"Seriously?" The venom in his voice couldn't be mistaken for anything but, and his eyes filled with fury. Fear crept into Rico's gut. Suddenly, he knew what Brian was about to say, and there was nothing he could do to stop him. "It's about you being a fucking rapist, asshole! Now let go of me!"

Great. Just what he needed—for the damn kid to announce Rico's past in his place of business. At least the few regulars sitting at the bar knew Rico well enough that they would have difficulty believing what they just heard. But that didn't stop everyone in the place from staring at them in shock.

He let go of the struggling teen. "I'm not—"

"Bullshit! Stay away from my father!"

Brian stormed out the door before Rico could say anything more.

"Fuck," he muttered, running a trembling hand down his face. He hadn't yet gotten around to telling Evan that piece of his personal history. In fact, he hoped they would've been a lot farther into their relationship before he needed to confess his past. Now, he wondered if he'd ever get a chance. The last thing he wanted was to see the disgust in Evan's eyes that he just saw in his son's.

"Guess he found out about your arrest and didn't dig further to find the truth." Rico turned to face Jeremy Smith, a retired SFPD detective who witnessed one of the worst weeks in Rico's life. The now gray-haired man hadn't been involved in the rape case but learned about it after another horrible event Rico lived through. "I heard the yelling from the bathroom. Otherwise, I would've stepped in and set the kid straight." His voice carried throughout the bar, letting everyone else know that Rico wasn't what he'd just been accused of being.

"Thanks, Jer."

"You're dating his father?" When Rico nodded, Jeremy placed a reassuring hand on his shoulder. "Talk to the guy—he'll understand. And if he doesn't, he's an ass."

Feeling numb, Rico nodded again, then returned to the receipts and began piling them up in random order. Just thinking about telling Evan what happened years ago had Rico's stomach threatening to rebel against the sandwich he'd eaten for lunch. He was so afraid Evan wouldn't give him a chance to explain or believe him when he did.

Six

"Rico, is everything okay? I've left a few messages. Please call me when you get a chance." Evan disconnected the call and sighed in exasperation, hating that his voicemail sounded desperate.

After he had to cancel their date on Thursday, he thought everything was okay, but when he called Rico on his break, he got the man's voicemail with no callback. Evan shrugged it off, thinking the bar might have been busy. But when he left another message on Rico's voicemail the next day, asking if they were still on for that evening, he received a text back saying Rico needed to cancel, but with no further explanation. It was now Sunday morning, and Evan still hadn't spoken to him. He only got the occasional text saying Rico was busy and couldn't take time from the bar to see Evan.

The disappointment rolling through him physically hurt. Even though his relationship with Rico was new, he honestly thought they had something good developing between them. But it seemed like he was getting the brush off now, and he didn't know why.

"Morning."

Evan looked up from the kitchen table to see Brian stroll in. The boys slept over at Evan's place last night because Susan had gone on another date with the new man in her life. When Evan spoke to her on the phone yesterday, she sounded happy. It made him smile because that's what he wanted for her, but after hanging up, a flash of jealousy went through him. He thought Rico was special—what they had was special—but was it just a fling and wishful thinking on Evan's part?

Maybe he'd go to the Cock & Bull later to see if he could corner Rico there and find out what was going on. Had Evan done something wrong? He didn't think so.

God, this sucks. The first guy you actually want to date—like seriously, date—and you start falling for him, and then things go to shit.

As Brian sat at the table, Evan tried to paste on a smile. "Good morning. How'd you sleep?" A lazy shrug was his answer. Getting to his feet, he opened the refrigerator. "Bacon and eggs or pancakes?"

"Bacon, eggs, and pancakes?" Mark said hopefully as the fourteen-year-old appeared in the doorway. "Hash browns, too, if you have some."

Evan laughed. It'd been a long time since he was a

teenager, eating everything in sight, but having two growing boys meant he had to keep the fridge and pantry stocked for whenever they visited or spent the night. "Three hungry-man specials coming up."

Pushing the MIA Rico from his mind for the moment, Evan gathered the ingredients he needed to make his kids a big breakfast.

The pounding on his condo door gave him a headache, and Rico wished whoever it was would just give up already. His hopes were dashed, though, when he heard the lock disengage, and Scout pushed the door open, then closed it behind him. He was dressed in jeans, a Turner Continental T-shirt, and sneakers, which meant that today, he was free of any obligations that required him to wear a suit, or at least dress pants and a TC polo shirt.

Rico scowled at him. "I gave you a key for emergencies only."

"This is an emergency," he replied dryly, dropping down on the couch across from the recliner Rico spent the day sulking in. "You see, the man who's like a brother to me is fucking up the best thing that's ever happened to him, and I need to know why."

"What are you talking about?"

Scout frowned. "Alex and I stopped by the bar, and Gino told us you've been home sick the past three days.

Then, before I have a chance to say 'What the fuck?' because you didn't say anything to me about being sick, Alex gets a phone call from Evan, asking if he knows if you're okay. He's worried because he hasn't been able to get you on the phone. And when he tried to stop by, he couldn't find you at the bar, and you wouldn't answer your phone when the concierge called to see if it was okay for them to send him up. So, tell me, brother, *what the fuck* is going on?"

He rolled his bloodshot eyes and sipped the beer he cracked open a few minutes earlier—his third of the day. "It wasn't working out. End of story."

"Bullshit, Rico. This is me you're talking to. You floated around on cloud nine for two weeks—something I've never seen you do—and now, suddenly, it's over? What happened?"

Rico considered lying to his best friend, but he owed it to him to be honest. "His kid stopped by the bar the other day and warned me off his dad."

Scout's eyes narrowed. "What? Why'd he do that?"

"He doesn't want his father dating an accused rapist."

"Aw, fuck. He seriously said that?"

"Yup—announced it to the whole damn bar." Rico sighed. "At least it was almost empty at the time, and Jeremy cleared things up for anyone listening, but not until after Brian left."

"Brian? That's the kid's name?

"Yeah."

"Okay. So, I take it you haven't told Evan about all that yet."

"Nope." He picked at the label on the beer bottle. "It's not exactly dinner conversation or something to bring up before or after fucking each other's brains out."

"Jesus, Rico. You're innocent. That was proven. You didn't even go to trial. Explain what happened to Evan. He'll understand."

"You didn't see that kid's face, man. I don't think there's a thing I can say to make him believe I didn't rape that girl."

Scout jumped up, grabbed the beer bottle from Rico's hand, slammed it onto the coffee table, and then got into Rico's face. "You. Did. Not. Rape. That. Girl. You have the proof you didn't. If that kid doesn't believe you, then so what?"

"Don't you see? If he doesn't believe me, how can I have a relationship with his father, knowing that the kid will always look at me and think the worst?" Hot tears scalded his cheeks. He tried to erase his past, but it still kept coming back to haunt him.

"Then make him believe you. Get the fucking file and shove it into the kid's face. Stop thinking you don't deserve to be happy because of what happened, Rico. It wasn't your fault. Stop blaming yourself."

Taking a deep breath, Rico held a thick file in the crook of his arm and knocked on the door to Evan's apartment with his free hand. It was two days since Scout tore him a new asshole for fucking things up, and Rico finally summoned the courage to try to fix what he broke. He picked up the phone several times to call Evan before convincing himself he needed to do it in person. Thankfully, Evan texted him his address last week when they were supposed to have dinner there.

He heard muffled voices behind the door, and then it swung open. When Brian spotted Rico standing there, his face reddened as he frowned. "What the fuck are you doing here?"

"Brian!" Evan's voice came from farther inside the apartment. "Who're you talking to like that?" There was a pause, and then Evan appeared behind his son, who had rage rolling off him in waves.

Evan's brow furrowed. "Rico? What're you doing here?"

"We need to talk."

"Um, okay."

He went to brush by Brian and move out into the hall, but Rico stopped him and gestured toward the teen. "With Brian."

Evan glanced back and forth between Brian and Rico, who were in a Mexican standoff—neither willing to back down. "What's going on? You two have met before?"

Stepping forward, Rico forced the teenager to move

back into the apartment. Evan stood there, confusion etched on his face as Rico closed the door. "Your son came to visit me at the bar the other day."

"What? Why?"

Rico's gaze stayed pinned to Brian's angry one. "To tell me to leave you alone."

"What? Why would you do that, Bri?"

As Rico expected, the kid exploded. "Because you deserve better than someone who's a fucking rapist, Dad!"

Evan's eyes grew wide as he stared at his son. "Wha—"

"Evan, sit down." Rico put a gentle hand on the other man's shoulder. "Both of you, please, while I explain what's going on."

Still stunned, Evan nodded and grabbed Brian's arm, turning him toward the living room. Once they sat on the couch, Rico glanced around. "Is Mark here? He should probably hear this too."

Evan shook his head. "He's at a study group tonight."

Placing the folder on the coffee table, Rico took a seat on a recliner, leaned forward, and rested his elbows on his knees. "Brian found out I was arrested when I was twenty years old. I was accused of raping a sixteen-year-old girl." Two sets of eyes were on him— one filled with hostility, the other with shock. Swallowing hard, he continued. "I worked at a coffee shop—one of two jobs I was holding down to pay for college—and this teenage girl came in often. Sometimes with her friends and sometimes alone. It was a Tuesday. March twenty-ninth." That day would forever be etched in his mind. "She came in after school and got the iced coffee she always ordered. It was raining out, and she had an umbrella and her book bag. Even after all these years, I can still see her so clearly in my mind. She used to flirt with me, not realizing I was gay. I got better tips if I flirted back with people, no matter their gender, so most of our customers didn't know if I was gay or not.

"Anyway, after she left, it was the end of my shift. I was exhausted because I'd been up late studying for a test, so I went home. I was still living with my aunt and uncle at the time. Everyone was either at work or school, so no one could confirm I was there." His gaze fell onto Brian. "I already told your dad that my folks were killed in a car accident when I was a sophomore in high school—my aunt and uncle took me in."

The kid didn't seem affected by that bit of information, so Rico shifted his gaze to Evan, who listened intently. "On her way home, the girl was attacked, raped, and left for dead in an alley not far from the coffee shop. She was in a coma for a few days, and when she woke up, she told the cops I was the one who did it. She even picked me out of a photo lineup."

He took a deep, ragged breath and let it out slowly. It had been a long time since he'd told his story to anyone. "So, they arrested me and charged me with rape and attempted murder. I was fingerprinted, photographed, and tossed into a cell. From there, I was arraigned and taken to jail because the bail was set too high for my aunt and uncle to get me out. I was in there two days before my friend Scout found out.

"His parents had known me for years and knew I was gay and wouldn't have . . . wouldn't have raped anyone, especially not a girl. They hired a lawyer and bailed me out of jail. It was three weeks later that the DA's office got the lab results back on the rape kit done on the girl at the hospital. I wasn't a match—not even close—and all the charges were dropped.

"What they think happened was, since I was the last person she interacted with before the brutal attack, her mind focused on me because I was the only one she could remember talking to that day. They eventually connected the suspect to three other rapes before they caught him. He's serving life in prison because one of the girls he raped and beat didn't make it."

Evan reached over and grasped Rico's hand. Rico held onto it like a lifeline. His eyes watered when he realized Evan believed him. Unfortunately, Rico wasn't done yet. "There's more. A year after the attack, the girl committed suicide. She left two letters behind—one for her parents and one for me. She couldn't handle the aftermath of the rape anymore, nor the fact that she almost sent an innocent man to prison. She begged me to forgive her."

"My God." Evan took several deep breaths before

turning to Brian. "How did you find out about the arrest?"

The teen's gaze was now on the floor. "I did one of those background checks on him and Steve, the guy Mom's dating. It said he'd been arrested."

"That information's still out there for anyone to see even though the charges were dropped?" Evan's eyes were wide in disbelief and outrage.

Rico nodded. "Yeah, but it's not supposed to be. Not long after Christina—that was the girl's name—she killed herself, I started seeing a guy. He did one of those searches, too, after our third date. Apparently, the record wasn't expunged like it was supposed to be. The guy got a few of his buddies together and came after me to dole out some justice. They wouldn't listen when I tried to tell them it was a false arrest. Beat the crap out of me and put me in the hospital for a few days. They didn't think I'd have the courage to press charges, but I did, and they did prison time. My record was finally expunged, but once it's on one of those random background-check sites, it's almost impossible to get it off."

The hand still holding his squeezed. "Shit. How the hell did you get through all that and come out okay?"

Rico snorted, then wiped his wet eyes with his free hand. "My family and Scout. My best friend was there for all of it, and I'll be forever grateful to him." He pointed to the file on the coffee table. "Brian, all the proof of my innocence is in there. I've kept everything in case I ever needed it. I care about your dad—he means a lot to me. I was going to tell him about all this at some point, but it's a heavy subject, and I just hadn't found the right time to drop it on him. But now that it's out, I don't want this hanging like a dark cloud over our relationship. Can we put it behind us?"

When the teen lifted his head, tears rolled down his cheeks. "I'm—I'm sorry, Dad. I thought I was protecting you."

Releasing Rico's hand, Evan pulled Brian into a tight embrace. "It's okay, son. It's okay."

When he glanced over his shoulder, Rico's gaze met his, and he nodded. It *was* going to be okay.

Seven

E van held Rico's hand as they strode up the front walkway leading to the home in Oakland he and Susan bought from her parents fifteen years ago when the older couple decided to retire to Arizona. At first, being a guest in the house he'd lived in with Susan and the boys was odd, but this time, it felt different. He looked forward to introducing his ex-wife to Rico. He would also meet the man Susan had dated for several weeks. Steve Probst was a radiologist and, according to Mark and Brian, a cool guy after he took the boys and Susan to a Giants game recently.

Things were better between Rico and Brian since Rico explained his past to the teen. Brian was worried he fucked up Evan and Rico's relationship, but the latter assured him they could move past the confrontation. Rico finally met Mark the other night when the four of them went out for pizza and a trip to a local driving range open after dark to hit some golf balls. Evan was pleasantly surprised to discover that Rico enjoyed the sport, and they had a tee time next Saturday with Scout and Alex at the Olympic Club, a private golf course and social club that hosted big tournaments like the U.S. Open.

Out of courtesy to Susan, Evan knocked on the door before pushing it open. She'd left it unlocked for them. "Sue?"

"In the kitchen," was her response.

He led Rico through the three-bedroom, two-bath house to the kitchen, where Susan stood at the stove, stirring something in a pot. Standing beside the island in the middle of the room was a tall, blond man with a mustache and goatee, mixing salad in a large bowl. Susan smiled broadly as she came over to give Evan a hug and a kiss on the cheek. Once again, he was reminded how lucky he was to have her in his life.

Pivoting, Evan gestured toward Rico. "Susan, this is Rico Demara."

Not surprisingly, she gave Rico a hug and a peck on the cheek too. "It's so nice to meet you finally. This is Steve Probst. Steve, this is Evan and Rico."

The men shook hands, and then Susan returned to the stove, telling Evan to get drinks for himself and Rico. Evan had been worried about Steve's reaction to not only having dinner with his girlfriend's ex-husband but also said ex-husband's boyfriend, but it didn't seem to faze the man. Within minutes, Rico and Steve were in a discussion about the Cock & Bull, which Steve had eaten a few times. Susan caught Evan's eye and winked at him, causing him to chuckle.

Yup, it looked like dinner would be a relaxing and enjoyable event.

After dinner, Rico excused himself when his cell phone rang. The number on the screen was for the Cock & Bull, and he went out the back door to the patio before connecting the call.

"Hello?"

"Hey, Rico, it's Gino."

Gino Demara was Rico's younger cousin, who he lived with after his parents were killed. Still trying to figure out what he wanted to do with his life, Gino flittered from one job to the next over the years but worked as a bartender at the C&B since it opened.

"What's up?"

"Just wanted to let you know Brett had to go to the hospital for stitches. He was filleting some fish and sliced himself up pretty good." Brett was their sous chef.

"Shit. Do you need me to come in?"

"Nah, I think we've got it covered. Only had to toss

the one fish. David was still here after his shift ended, so he took Brett to the hospital to get stitched up. Adam said they have everything under control in the kitchen." If the head chef needed help, he would ask for it.

"All right. Let me know if you need me to come in."

"I will, but I doubt it. Like I said—just wanted to give you a heads up."

"Thanks. Talk to you later."

It wasn't until after he disconnected the call that Rico noticed he wasn't alone on the patio. Mark sat in a chair near a fire pit, tapping away on his cell phone. Rico strode over and took the chair opposite him. He hadn't missed the way Mark eyed him during dinner. After the trip to the driving range the other night, things seemed to have shifted between them. Gone was the wariness in the teen's eyes, replaced by appreciative ogling. Rico was on the receiving end of those looks often, and he knew what they meant.

"Can I ask you something?" he said to Mark, who lifted his gaze to him. "You don't have to answer it if you don't want to."

The teen shrugged. "Sure."

"I get the feeling something's been on your mind lately. Do you want to talk about it?"

A long pause followed as Mark debated whether he wanted to go down the road Rico suspected was in front of him. Finally, he nodded. "How did you know you were gay?"

Rico leaned back in the chair and casually placed his ankle on the opposite knee. "I was just about your age when I figured it out. I'd look at girls and realize they didn't stir up these feelings that I got when I looked at guys." He waited a moment before asking, "Is that what's happening with you?"

Mark's cheeks reddened before he nodded. "Yeah. It kinda scares me, though."

"Because you're afraid you'll lose some friends and family members if you come out?"

"Uh-huh. That's what happened to my dad. Some of his friends dumped him, and my mom's sister and her family stopped talking to him afterward. They get this disgusted look on their faces when Dad's name is mentioned. It pisses my mom off—pisses me off too."

"I get it. Being gay isn't always easy, even in this day and age." Rico sighed heavily. "But if you lose anyone because of who you're attracted to, then those people weren't worth having in your life anyway. But you've got a great man to look up to. Your dad will always be there for you. Not every gay kid has a parent who truly gets it. You're lucky. And if you have questions you're embarrassed to ask your dad, you can always come to me."

Mark shyly dropped his gaze to the ground. "Thanks."

"You're welcome."

Movement out of the corner of his eye had Rico turning his head to see Evan quietly watching them. It was apparent he'd overheard their conversation when he mouthed, "I love you. Thank you," to Rico. Not wanting Mark to know his secret was out until he was ready for it to be, Rico just winked at Evan and smiled. When they were alone, there would be plenty of time to let Evan know how much Rico loved him too.

Eight

Three weeks later . . .

Evan double-checked his bowtie before leaving his bedroom. Out in the living room, Rico chatted with Mark and Brian, and once again, he looked sexy as hell in his tuxedo. This one was all black but also fit him perfectly.

Tonight was an award show, and both the sportscast teams of Bentley & Barrett and Morrison & Savage were nominated for awards. Everyone involved in getting the two shows on the air would be in attendance, and Evan had invited Rico to come as his date. It was the first time Evan would be open about his sexual orientation at a work-related event, and he was a bit nervous about it. A few people he trusted knew he was out and proud, but there were others to whom he hadn't felt comfortable exposing himself.

"How do I look?" He spun around in a circle.

"Good," Mark and Brian said simultaneously, not even inspecting him beyond a quick glance. His older son flipped through the options on Netflix while the younger one texted someone on his phone.

Rico gave Evan a suggestive smile. "I'd say better than good. Ready to go?"

He patted his pockets. "Got my wallet, keys, and phone. Yup, I'm ready. Guys, don't eat everything in the pantry and fridge, all right? Leave me something to eat this week. I'll see you in the morning."

Brian gave him a thumbs-up. "Good luck, Dad."

A few minutes later, they were in Rico's car, a black Dodge Charger that Evan had been lucky enough to drive a few times. He loved the sleek vehicle that fit its owner to a T.

It didn't take them long to arrive at the Terra Gallery, where the award show was held. Evan chuckled when a valet hungrily eyed Rico's car.

"Better not be a scratch on it when I get it back," Rico muttered to him as they strode into the venue. "Or drool."

The lobby buzzed with people representing all the radio stations in the Bay Area. The first person Evan spotted from KCXN was Lily Albert. When he introduced her to Rico, he almost choked as she grinned with amusement and asked Rico what shoe size he wore.

Soon, others from the station joined them,

including Eric Bentley, Tom Barrett, Ray Morrison, and Dave Savage. The first three were with their wives, while Savage had some busty, blonde bimbo on his arm. He had a penchant for women who didn't have much in the brains department. When Evan introduced Rico to everyone, he wasn't surprised that Savage didn't extend his hand for Rico to shake like the others had. But, then again, Rico hadn't reached out either.

As flutes of champagne passed by on trays, Rico snatched two glasses and gave one to Evan before lifting his own and gesturing to the two sportscast teams. "Good luck tonight, gentlemen."

Everyone but Savage smiled and thanked him.

About fifteen minutes of chitchat later, the overhead lights flashed once, an indication that the attendees should head into the main ballroom and find their seats. Evan put his hand on Rico's arm. "I'm just going to run to the men's room."

Rico nodded. "Sure. I'll wait for you here."

A few men exited as Evan walked into the upscale lounge. He'd just finished at the urinal when the door opened, and Savage strode in, spotted Evan, and scoffed. "Should've known you were a faggot, but I didn't expect you to flaunt your fucking boy toy in everyone's faces."

Rage flowed through Evan. He didn't care what people thought of him, but he'd be damned if he let this asshole talk about Rico that way. "Screw you, Savage."

"No, thanks. I don't take it up the ass like you do.

You can forget about working on my show ever again. I'll demand a new sound tech on Monday, and you'll be looking for a new job if I have my way."

Before Evan could respond, a toilet flushed, and the door to one of the stalls slammed open. Both men were shocked to see the president of KCXN stroll out. Bishop Kane was a good-looking man in his early fifties. His salt-and-pepper hair was neatly styled, and his sharp green eyes narrowed as he walked right up to Savage and got in his face. "Actually, Savage, you're the one who'll be out of a job come Monday. I don't tolerate gay bashing or any other kind of sexual harassment at my station. Consider this the end of your career at KCXN. I'll have payroll mail your final check because I don't want you stepping one foot in my station ever again."

If Evan weren't so stunned, he would've laughed at how pale Savage was. The bastard tried to recover, though. "You can't fire me! I have a contract!"

"You should've read it more carefully before you signed it because sexual harassment is an offense that can void it. Now, get out of my face before I have you thrown out of here."

Now red-faced and looking like he was about to blow a gasket, Savage spun around and stormed out of the restroom, yelling something about them hearing from his lawyer.

Mr. Kane didn't say anything to Evan until after they washed and dried their hands. He then held one out to Evan. "My son is gay and has been happily married to his husband for five years now. If you have any problems with Savage outside the station after this, I expect you to let me know."

Evan shook his hand. "Y-yes, sir. Thank you."

"Let's go enjoy the show, shall we?"

Nine

Eight months later . . .

E van sat in the broadcast booth, rubbing his hands against his pants. His palms were sweaty, and so was his brow. Usually, he was on the other side of the window that separated the sound techs' room from the booth where the sportscasters did their shows. But today, he would talk during a live broadcast and hope it was one of the most incredible days of his life.

When he first came up with the idea of proposing on the air to Rico, he immediately dismissed it. But the more it ran through his mind, the more he thought it was romantic. He just hoped Rico agreed.

Every morning, before taking the elevator down to go to work, Rico sat in his recliner, playing around on his computer and listening to Eric Bentley and Tom

Barrett talk about what was going on in sports. When Evan asked Eric and Tom if they would let him get on the air with them and ask Rico to marry him, they were all for it as long as it was okay with Mr. Kane. The older man was thrilled to have his station help with the proposal.

So, now, Evan had another few minutes before Eric and Tom wrapped up their show and gave him the go-ahead. It was almost ten o'clock, and Rico would walk out the door of his condo in a half hour, so the timing was perfect—Evan prayed.

Fear rattled around in his head. What if Rico was in the shower and completely missed when Evan put his heart on the line? What if he said no?

Evan fidgeted in his chair as Eric thanked their sponsors and said, "We have a special guest here in the broadcast booth. KCXN's own Evan Calhoun—the sound tech for the Bentley & Barrett show. How're you doing, Evan?"

He licked his lips and swallowed hard before replying. "I'm—I'm good."

"Glad to hear it. We've got your caller on the line and are ready to go. Let's just get him in on this conversation." Eric hit a button on the multi-line phone. "Rico, you there?"

"I am. Although, I'm not sure why."

Eric pointed to Evan, who leaned closer to the microphone. "Hey, babe, it's me."

"Evan? Hey, what's going on?"

He took a deep breath, and all the words he wanted to say fled his mind except for "Will you marry me?"

There was a long pause, and then Tom's eyes widened as he glanced around. "Rico, you still there?"

Evan thought his heart skipped a few beats before he heard, "Seriously, Evan? You're doing this over the radio, with me miles away and unable to kiss you when I said yes?"

There was an even longer pause because, this time, Evan was speechless. He couldn't figure out if Rico's answer was yes or not.

Eric chuckled. "His jaw hit the floor, folks. Hey, Rico, does this mean you're saying yes? You'll marry Evan?"

When Evan heard his lover's voice next, it wasn't through the speakers but, instead, from directly behind him. "Turn around, Ev."

Shaking, he did as ordered, finding Rico down on one knee. Somehow, they managed to get him into the broadcast booth without Evan noticing. He just stared at the man he loved, seeing that love returned to him.

"Rico pulled a fast one, everyone. He's not miles away. He's in our studio and down on one knee, with a ring box in his hand, and Evan's still gaping in shock."

"Tom," Rico said without taking his gaze off Evan. "We don't need a play-by-play here."

"Well, it is a sports show, and we can't have dead air, so start talking, dude."

He chuckled, then took Evan's hand. "When I asked

Tom and Eric if I could propose to you during their show, they said they would come up with a plan to get you on the air. I just didn't know you would propose to me too. You threw me off my game there for a few seconds, but now I'm back on track. I never thought I'd meet someone who took my breath away just by looking at me. But you do, Ev. You're the other half of my soul I never thought I'd find." He opened the small black box to reveal a gold and platinum band with diamonds embedded in the center of it. "Will you marry me?"

Evan wiped away the tears rolling down his cheeks before nodding. "Yes, but just remember who asked first."

Smiling, Rico got to his feet and pulled Evan up with him, smashing his mouth down on his. The kiss was fierce and demanding. Both barely noticed when Tom said, "And that's the end of our show, everyone. We'll be back tomorrow with more sports and a newly engaged sound tech."

Lying on his side, Rico rested his head on Evan's bare shoulder, entwined their hands together, and ran his thumb over the ring on Evan's left hand. He spent weeks searching for just the right ring, often dragging Scout and Alex along. When he finally spotted one he loved, he took photos of it and sent them to Mark and

Brian via text. Both had given their seals of approval. "Do you like it?"

"I love it. Do you like yours?"

After Evan got over the shock of Rico showing up at the station and throwing his own proposal for a loop, he pulled a box from his pocket and presented a ring to his new fiancé. Rico held his other hand up and stared at the matte-finish platinum ring with black diamonds set into a channel in the middle of the band. "It's perfect."

When they stepped out of the broadcast booth and into a large office, where the sportscasters' and reporters' desks were, it was filled with people from all the different departments that made up KCXN. The applause was deafening, and Bishop Kane was the first to shake their hands and congratulate them. He then gave Evan the rest of the day off.

Evan's coworkers surprised them with a cake and champagne, so the newly engaged couple got stuck there longer than Rico had intended. In the meantime, Brian called Evan from the University of Southern California, where he was in his first year of studies for broadcast journalism, to congratulate his father and Rico. He knew about both intended proposals and streamed the Bentley & Barrett show to hear them live. Mark planned to do the same while in study hall that morning.

Evan's younger son would join them, Susan and Steve, who were still together, newlyweds Scout and

Alex, Magnus, Rex, and several other close friends and family members that night at the Cock & Bull to celebrate.

It was an hour before Rico had finally been able to get them out of the radio station. They couldn't make it back to his condo fast enough for him, but somehow, he managed to get them there in record time, where they stripped each other before tumbling into bed and making love.

"What do you think of a June wedding?" Evan asked as he nuzzled the top of Rico's head.

"Isn't that a little cliché?" When Evan shrugged, Rico rolled on top of him, straddling his hips. He grasped Evan's wrists and pinned them to either side of his head. "What do you say we elope this weekend?"

Evan's eyes grew wide. "This—this weekend? Are you nuts?"

He kissed his fiancé. "Nope. Just want to make you mine as soon as I can."

"I'm already yours. But if you want to elope, then let's do it."

"Good, because Kane already gave you next week off for a wedding present."

"What? When did he do that?"

Rico nipped Evan's jaw, then licked away the sting, eliciting a moan from him. Rico's cock hardened again, getting ready for a second round of hot, raunchy sex. "Last week at the award show, when I asked if he could sign off on a vacation week for you without letting you know."

In a flash, Evan switched their positions, putting Rico flat on his back and slamming their mouths together. Their tongues danced around each other, and their hands were everywhere, touching, caressing, loving.

"I love you," Evan murmured against Rico's lips before he shifted and pushed himself down the bed, licking, nipping, and sucking on the smooth skin of Rico's chest and abdomen. He settled himself between Rico's legs. Grabbing the bottle of lube from the nightstand, he coated his throbbing cock with the slick liquid. "Hold your legs up for me, babe."

When Rico hooked his arms under his knees and pulled them toward his chest, Evan moaned at the sight of the puckered hole eagerly waiting for him. Rico's cock was hard and long against the trail of hair that ran down the center of his belly to his groin. Pre-cum seeped from the slit.

Evan made quick work of prepping Rico before lining the tip of his cock up to the entrance of the place he called his home. Evan never felt he was where he was supposed to be more than when he was deep inside Rico. After both were tested months ago, they got rid of the condoms once and for all. The heat Evan felt when Rico's body engulfed him was unlike anything he'd ever experienced.

"Fuck me, Ev. Please." Rico's eyes begged him as much as his mouth did. "Need you. Hard, fast."

Evan kept his gaze on Rico's face as he slid inside the man's body, trying to control the urge to thrust deep on the first pass. With short thrusts, he gained ground until he was as deep as possible. Rico gasped, moaned, and cursed as his channel adjusted to the thick intrusion. His walls were so tight around Evan's shaft that it was a wonder Evan didn't blow his load without further stimulation.

Once the tension eased from Rico's body and he was confident he wouldn't hurt him, Evan began to pound into him as if his life depended on it. Sweat poured off him as he strived to bring them the bliss they both craved. With every forward thrust of Evan's hips, Rico grunted as he took the punishing rhythm without complaint.

Evan leaned down and kissed the mouth he dreamed about every night, but he panted so hard that he had to back off to pull oxygen into his lungs. When the telltale tingling began racing down his spine, he wrapped his hand tightly around Rico's cock and tugged with the same pace as his hips rocking back and forth.

"Shit!" Rico yelled when his body went rigid. He came with such force that he shook. The spurts of hot cum on Evan's hand and Rico's ass clenching around his cock was all it took for Evan to follow him into orgasmic bliss.

As they lay in a sated heap, Rico ran his hand up and down Evan's spine. "I love you, baby."

Evan smiled into the crook of Rico's neck. It may have taken him thirty-eight years to get there, but he was finally where he belonged. "I love you too."

I hope you enjoyed Rico and Evan's story. Next, check out *The Sugarplum Fairy: An MM Holiday Novella*.

Rico's Playlist

Listen to Rico's Playlist on Spotify

"When You Close Your Eyes" - Night Ranger

"Your Wildest Dreams" - The Moody Blues

"Any Way You Want It" - Journey

"Take a Chance on Me" - ABBA

"Can't Keep a Good Man Down" - Alabama

"My Kinda Lover" - Billy Squier

"If You Want My Love" - Cheap Trick

"Believe" - Cher

"I Woke Up in Love this Morning" - The Partridge Family

"Sharing the Night Together" - Dr. Hook

"Two Less Lonely People in the World" - Air Supply

"Think I'm in Love" - Eddie Money

"I'd Really Love to See You Tonight" - England Dan & John Ford Coley

"Do You Believe In Love" - Huey Lewis & The News

(WITH **13** OTHER AUTHORS)

Jack Be Nimble: A Trident Security-Related Short Story

***DEIMOS SERIES

Handling Haven: Special Forces: Operation Alpha

Cheating the Devil: Special Forces: Operation Alpha

TRIDENT SECURITY OMEGA TEAM SERIES

Mountain of Evil

A Dead Man's Pulse

Forty Days & One Knight

DOMS OF THE COVENANT SERIES

Double Down & Dirty

Entertaining Distraction

Knot a Chance

Finding His Forever

BLACKHAWK SECURITY SERIES

Tuff Enough

Blood Bound

MASTER KEY SERIES

Master Key Resort

Master Cordell

HAZARD FALLS SERIES

Don't Fight It

Don't Shoot the Messenger

Cock & Bull Series

Scout

Rico

Malone Brothers Series

Her Secret

Her Sleuth

Largo Ridge Series

Cold Feet

Antelope Rock Series
(Co-authored with J.B. Havens)

Wannabe in Wyoming

Wistful in Wyoming

Award-Winning Standalone Books

The Road to Solace

Scattered Moments in Time: A Collection of Short Stories & More

Standalone Books

Sweet Revenge (A Novella)

The Sugarplum Fairy (A Novella)

***The Bid on Love Series

(with 7 other authors!)

Going, Going, Gone: Book 2

*****The Collective: Season Two**

(with 7 other authors!)

Angst: Book 7

*****Special Collections**

Trident Security Series: Volume I

Trident Security Series: Volume II

Trident Security Series: Volume III

Trident Security Series: Volume IV

Trident Security Series: Volume V

Trident Security Series: Volume VI

About Samantha Cole

USA Today Bestselling Author and Award-Winning Author Samantha Cole is a retired policewoman and former paramedic. Using her life experiences and training, she strives to find the perfect mix of suspense and romance for her readers to enjoy.

Awards:

Wannabe in Wyoming (co-authored by J.B. Havens) won the bronze medal in the 2021 Readers' Favorite Awards in the General Romance category.

Scattered Moments in Time, won the gold medal in the 2020 Readers' Favorite Awards in the Fiction Anthology category.

The Road to Solace (formerly *The Friar*), won the silver medal in the 2017 Readers' Favorite Awards in the Contemporary Romance category.

Samantha has over thirty-five books published throughout several different series as well as a few standalone novels. A full list can be found on her website.

Sexy Six-Pack's Sirens Group on Facebook
Website: www.samanthacoleauthor.com
Newsletter: www.geni.us/SCNews

facebook.com/SamanthaColeAuthor

instagram.com/samanthacoleauthor

bookbub.com/profile/samantha-a-cole

goodreads.com/SamanthaCole

amazon.com/Samantha-A-Cole/e/B00X53K3X8